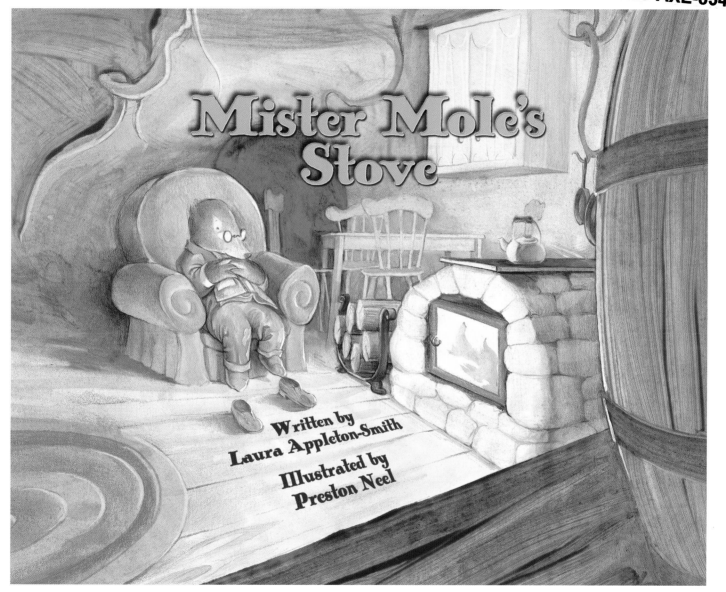

Mister Mole's Stove

Written by
Laura Appleton-Smith

Illustrated by
Preston Neel

Laura Appleton-Smith was born and raised in Vermont and holds a degree in English from Middlebury College. Laura is a primary school teacher who has combined her talents in creative writing and her experience in early childhood education to create *Books to Remember*. Laura lives in New Hampshire with her husband, Terry.

Preston Neel was born in Macon, Georgia. Greatly inspired by Dr. Seuss, he decided to become an artist at the age of four. Preston's advanced art studies took place at the Academy of Art College San Francisco. Now Preston pursues his career in art with the hope of being an inspiration himself, particularly to children who want to explore their endless bounds.

A Book to Remember™
Published by Flyleaf Publishing

For orders or information, contact us at **(800) 449-7006**.
Please visit our website at **www.flyleafpublishing.com**

Eighth Edition 2/20
Library of Congress Catalog Card Number: 2004094987
Softcover ISBN-13: 978-1-929262-24-3
Printed and bound in the USA at Worzalla Publishing, Stevens Point, WI

For Aleks and Luka.

LAS

—

To Riley, Cole, Noli, Fiona, Jeremy and Evie,
and to Terra, Ella, Jordan, Erich, Julia, Annie, Jack and Ki-Ki;
the little treasure hunters at the shore the summer of 2004.

PN

Mister Mole lived in a hole at the top of a windswept slope.

He dug his home in the sand with his little mole hands long ago when he was just a lad.

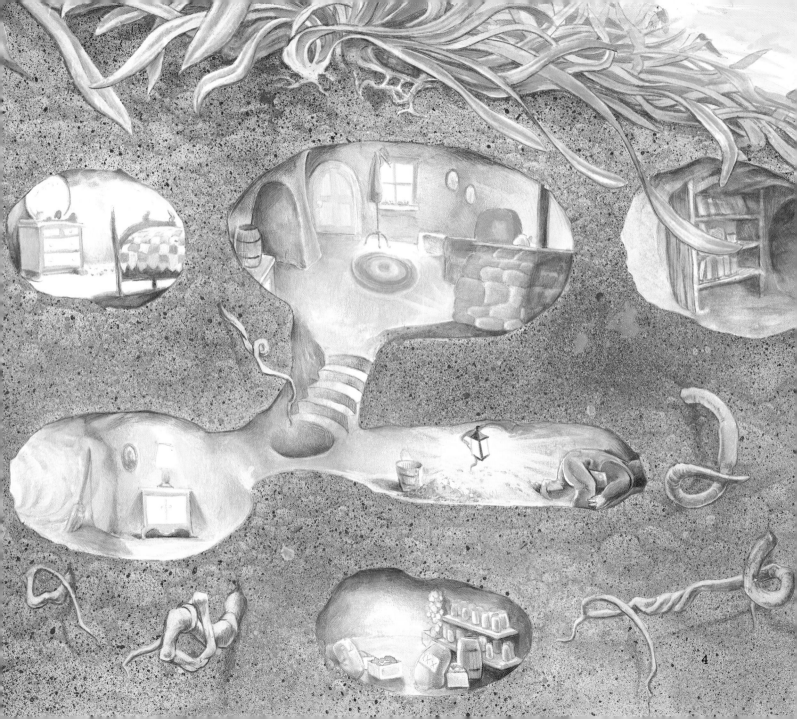

In his hole Mister Mole had woven a bed
with twigs and grass and rope.

He stuffed it with fluff and bits of fabric and rug.
It was a nest that kept him snug.

6

But what made Mister Mole's hole different
from the rest of the holes on the slope was his stove.

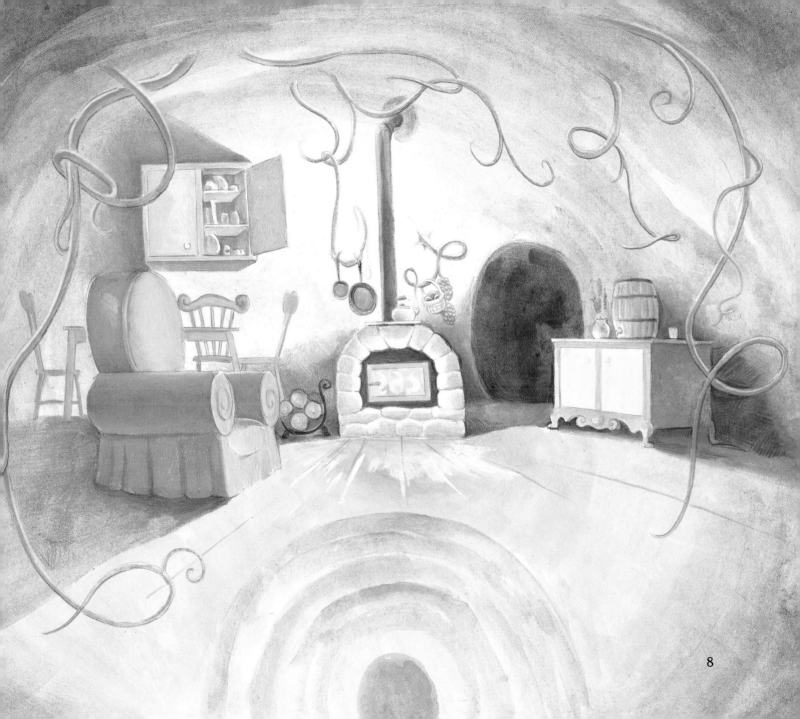

When Mister Mole was a strong lad, he had
dragged stone after stone up from the cove.

Mister Mole's hole was dug in a sand bank where
no stones existed, but the cove was filled with rocks.

The rest of the moles on the slope had poked fun at him. "You are nuts," they joked, as Mister Mole dragged up stone after stone with a sack and a rope.

But Mister Mole did not take note.

He had a plan to construct a stove that would warm
his home for the rest of his days.

Long ago he had stacked stones and mud
to construct a stove that kept him warm and snug.

Now, as Mister Mole sat and warmed his old bones,
he was glad that he had dragged those stones.

"Just remembering dragging you stones
    up from the cove makes me want a nap,"
    old Mister Mole joked as he stoked his stove.

Warm and relaxed, he fluffed his bed
and dozed off for a nap.

18

When Mister Mole awoke from his nap
his nose was filled with smoke.

He jumped up and opened his hole.
As the smoke drifted out he spotted the problem…

One stone in his stove had broken.

20

What was Mister Mole to do?

He felt too old to drag stones up the slope,
but he had to cope, so he set off with his
old sack and rope.

Mister Mole slipped and stumbled as he slid down the slope.

He hoped that his old bones would not end up broken too.

When Mister Mole got to the cove he inspected the stones—
too big, too little, too jagged to fit…

But then Mister Mole spotted the stone.
It sat in the bottom of the cove.
It was flat and the perfect fit.

That was it, but there was a problem—
Mister Mole was not the best swimmer…

But Mister Mole was not a mole to sit and mope.

He disrobed and dove in,
but no matter how he swam,
he could not get to the stone.

As Mister Mole pondered what to do next,
his friend the otter popped up and asked,

"My friend Mister Mole, why do you stand in the cove
frozen and wet?"

"In the bottom of the cove sits the perfect stone
that I must get to fix my stove, but I cannot swim to it,"
Mister Mole told him.

At that, Otter dove into the cove,
and as quick as he was in, he was back.

He had the stone in one hand and a clam in the other.

"I owe you," Mister Mole told Otter,
"but what can I do?"

"You can fix your stove with this perfect stone
and then you can warm me a pot of clam stew,"
Otter told him. "You help me and I help you.
That is what friends do."

So Mister Mole hopped on Otter's back
with his stone and his sack and his rope
and he rode back up the slope.

Then he fixed his stove…

40

And he fixed his friend the Otter a pot of clam stew.

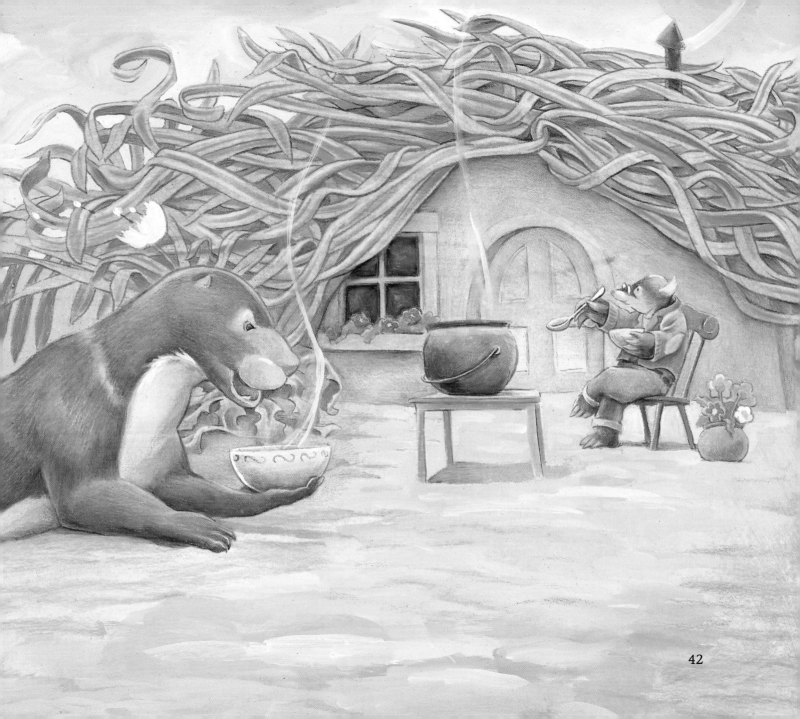

Prerequisite Skills

Single consonants and short vowels
Final double consonants **ff**, **gg**, **ll**, **nn**, **ss**, **tt**, **zz**
Consonant /k/ **ck**
/ng/ **n[k]**
Consonant digraphs /ng/ **ng**, /th/ **th**, /hw/ **wh**
Schwa /ə/ **a, e, i, o, u**
Long /ē/ **ee, y**
r-Controlled /ûr/ **er**
/ô/ **al, all**
/ul/ **le**
/d/ or /t/ **–ed**

Target Letter-Sound Correspondence	
Long /ō/ sound spelled **o_e**	
awoke	moles
bones	mope
broken	nose
cope	note
cove	owe
disrobed	poked
dove	rode
dozed	rope
hole	slope
holes	smoke
home	stoked
hoped	stone
joked	stones
Mole	stove
Mole's	those

High-Frequency Puzzle Words	
are	opened
could	other
days	out
do	so
down	take
for	there
from	they
he	to
how	too
into	want
lived	warm
made	warmed
makes	was
me	what
my	where
no	why
now	would
of	you
old	your
one	

Story Puzzle Words	
ago	remembering
friend	stew
friends	told
frozen	woven
relaxed	

Decodable Words

a	different	glad	lad	popped	strong
after	drag	got	little	pot	stuffed
and	dragged	grass	long	problem	stumbled
as	dragging	had	matter	quick	swam
asked	drifted	hand	Mister	rest	swim
at	dug	hands	mud	rocks	swimmer
back	end	help	must	rug	that
bank	existed	him	nap	sack	the
bed	fabric	his	nest	sand	then
best	felt	hopped	next	sat	this
big	filled	I	not	set	top
bits	fit	in	nuts	sit	twigs
bottom	fix	inspected	off	sits	up
but	fixed	is	on	slid	wet
can	flat	it	Otter	slipped	when
cannot	fluff	jagged	Otter's	snug	windswept
clam	fluffed	jumped	perfect	spotted	with
construct	fun	just	plan	stacked	
did	get	kept	pondered	stand	